K'S TOOTH

Diane Kredensor

ALADDIN

NEW YORK   LONDON   TORONTO   SYDNEY   NEW DELHI

This book is a work of fiction. Any references to historical events, real people, or real places are used fictitiously. Other names, characters, places, and events are products of the author's imagination, and any resemblance to actual events or places or persons, living or dead, is entirely coincidental.

ALADDIN

An imprint of Simon & Schuster Children's Publishing Division
1230 Avenue of the Americas, New York, New York 10020
First Aladdin edition March 2021
Copyright © 2015 by Diane Kredensor
All rights reserved, including the right of reproduction in whole or in part in any form.
ALADDIN and related logo are registered trademarks of Simon & Schuster, Inc.
For information about special discounts for bulk purchases, please contact
Simon & Schuster Special Sales at 1-866-506-1949 or business@simonandschuster.com.
The Simon & Schuster Speakers Bureau can bring authors to your live event. For more information
or to book an event contact the Simon & Schuster Speakers Bureau at 1-866-248-3049
or visit our website at www.simonspeakers.com.
Designed by Karina Granda
The illustrations for this book were rendered digitally.
The text of this book was set in Avenir.
Manufactured in China 0121 SCP
2 4 6 8 10 9 7 5 3 1
Library of Congress Control Number 2020937982
ISBN 978-1-5344-8107-7 (hc)
ISBN 978-1-5344-8106-0 (pbk)
ISBN 978-1-4814-2383-0 (eBook)

For Dana and Tina—my Pearls

—D. K.

CHAPTER ONE

This is Buck. He's a beaver.

Like most beavers, Buck had little ears,
a flat tail, thick brown fur, and
big front teeth.

Or in Buck's case, one big,
square front tooth.

Buck didn't like his tooth.

Not one bit.

That tooth ruined everything!

How Buck talked.

How Buck smiled.

How Buck ate.

It did make brushing his teeth easier,
but that was about it.

And now Buck's big, square tooth was about to
ruin the BIGGEST event of the year—

the Beaverton Talent Show.

No one in Beaverton would think of missing it.

Once, Jimmy Nagel blew such a big bubble, he flew up into a tree.

Everyone is still talking about when Charlie Lane wiggled his ears, tail, and nose while juggling four apples.

This year Buck and his friends were finally
old enough to enter the show.

Donald turned to Buck.

Buck looked from Donald
to Pearl to Marvin.
"It's a surprise," he said.

CHAPTER TWO

And it was a surprise.
Even to Buck.
He had no idea what his talent was.

Everything he tried to do ended in disaster.

Stilt walking.

Flute playing.

Whistling.

His tooth always got in the way.
Why did Buck have this silly tooth in the first place?

When Buck's tooth had started to grow, it looked different from everyone else's teeth in his family.

6 months

3 years

5 years

Everyone but . . .

his uncle Henry.

Buck looked exactly like him.

Uncle Henry was a famous sculptor. With his one
big tooth, he could sculpt just about anyone in Beaverton.

Sammy Squirrel
"AMAZING!"

BEAVERTON NEWS

Henry does it again!

Henry scuplts
squirrel.

Charlie Chipmunk
"INCREDIBLE!"

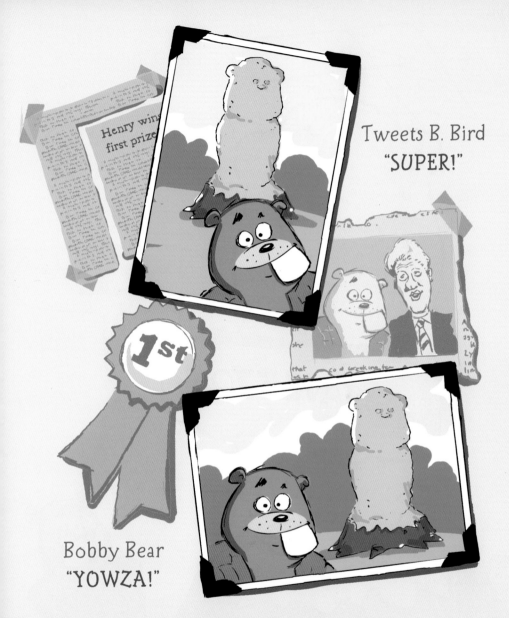

Tweets B. Bird "SUPER!"

Bobby Bear "YOWZA!"

Everyone thought Buck should
follow in Uncle Henry's footsteps.

Buck stopped.

For the first time in days, he smiled.

Buck was sure if he got rid of his tooth,
he would find his talent.

CHAPTER THREE

Buck hurried home and started planning
Operation Tooth Pull.

The next morning, he and his tooth were ready.

So long, Tooth. It's time to say good-bye!

Buck started with Plan A. He called his sisters.

Plan A didn't work.

Buck moved on to Plan B.

After opening . . .

thirty pecans,

twenty-two Brazil nuts,

and fifteen walnuts,

Buck's tooth still wouldn't budge.
No problem. There was always Plan C.

Buck was sure.

He closed his eyes. He took a deep breath
and bid farewell to his tooth.

Buck opened his eyes.
His tooth was still there.

Buck's tooth was still there.

No matter what Marvin said, *nothing* happened.

Operation Tooth Pull was officially a failure.

CHAPTER FOUR

Buck wanted to be alone. He went to
one of his favorite spots and crawled in.

Buck was starting to fall asleep when
he heard Pearl calling his name.

Buck didn't answer.

Finally, Buck spoke.

The surprise is that I have no talent.

All I have is a big tooth, and both of us are good at nothing.

That's not true, Buck.

Oh, really?

Have you seen me play the flute? Or walk on stilts? Or eat corn?

At first, Pearl was silent.
But before she left, she told Buck:

Once he was alone again, Buck couldn't stop thinking.

Everyone is going to grow up and leave me behind.

Pearl will be a famous singer.

CHAPTER FIVE

While everyone waited for the talent show to begin . . .

Uncle Henry wheeled
his statue to the back of the stage.

I think this is one of my greatest creations.

I've never worked so hard before.

Back at the log, Buck could hear
clapping, laughing, and cheering.
And then he heard singing. It was Pearl!

CHAPTER SIX

Frankie McSunders had just finished reciting "Casey at the Bat."

Fine job, Frankie.

And now Henry Broadtail invites you all to see his newest masterpiece.

The crowd gasped.

Uncle Henry smiled.

All eyes were on Buck.

Buck realized what he had said.
Then Buck realized what he had done.

And just like Pearl had said,

Buck's talent was right under his nose the whole time.